# A Creole Folktale

The Power of Love; The Magic of 3

Retold by

## Valencia Arceneaux

Illustrated by Simone Donatto

Archway Publishing books may be ordered through booksellers or by contacting:

Archway Publishing
1663 Liberty Drive
Bloomington, IN 47403
www.archwaypublishing.com
844-669-3957

ISBN: 978-1-6657-3885-9 (sc)
ISBN: 978-1-6657-3884-2 (hc)
ISBN: 978-1-6657-3886-6 (e)

Print information available on the last page.

Archway Publishing rev. date: 04/28/2023

# A Creole Folktale

The Power of Love; The Magic of 3

# Contents

# Acknowledgment

Sitting on the back steps of Mr. Anthony DeRouen, there was always a time for stories. My favorite story was about a mother and her three boys and a very smart, but hungry wolf. Over the years I retold the story to many young children with a few changes. Instead of a wolf as the antagonist, my "bad" character is an alligator. I added a lullaby at the end (passed on from several generations).

I wish to acknowledge Mr. DeRouen for his colorful stories, and his impact on my story-telling for all these years. This story must be given to all who believe in the magic of three and the power of love.

# Dedication

This book is dedicated to all those who believe in "passing it on."

And to all my children, grandchildren, and great grandchildren.

Once upon a time deep in the Louisiana swamps, there lived a mother and her three boys. Their papa was far away fighting in a war. Since Mama needed money to take care of the boys, she would leave them each morning and go off to work nearby.

"Comment sa va?" Mama inquired each morning upon waking the boys up. "Tres bien, eh vous?" they would reply. Then Mama would say, "Je vais tres bien, merci."

After a hot breakfast (sometimes oatmeal, sometimes beignets and other food), Mama would fix her lunch, kiss the boys, and remind them to keep the door locked until they heard her sing a special song.

This is her song:

"Bla blasie bla blasie moe,

Tackie nackie toe,

Tackie nackie toe,

Blasie blasie moe."

As soon as Mama left, the boys locked the door and started playing dominoes. They cleaned the house, and before you knew it, there came a knock at the door. The youngest boy ran to open the door, when the oldest shouted, "Don't open that door until we hear Mama's song!" "Mama, please sing your song," the middle boy called out. And so, Mama sang in her most beautiful voice. When she finished, they opened the door, and Mama walked in to give big hugs to all three boys.

After supper, the boys practiced writing, took their baths and got ready for bed. Mama reminded them to be very careful the next day because there was a sly, hungry alligator in the woods behind the house. Soon all were asleep.

The next morning after breakfast, Mama fixed her lunch, kissed the boys goodbye, and left for work. They played cards and hide-and-go-seek. Around lunch time, they heard a knock at the door. The middle boy forgot about the warning from Mama and just as he was about to open the door, the baby boy screamed, "Wait, wait!! What about the song?" At the last second, they hollered through the door, "Please sing for us, Mama."

With a scratchy, ugly voice, the alligator sang the song. (He had heard Mama sing the day before). The boys knew instantly that that was NOT Mama. "Leave right now, and don't you come back!!, they shouted. Of course the hungry, sly alligator slithered back into the woods, more determined than ever.

About three in the afternoon, they heard a knock again. This time the oldest boy went to the door and said, "Mama you need to sing your song very pretty". Even though Mama was curious about her son's comment, she sang in her most beautiful voice, "Bla blasie, Bla blasie mo…" Hearing this beautiful voice, they opened the door.

They were shaking as they told their mother about the alligator who tried to trick them at lunch. This upset Mama so much that she decided not to go to work the next day, but they needed food and other things, so the boys convinced her that they would be fine. They would be extra careful the next day. So finally the family retired for the night.

That night the alligator was desperately plotting to get into the house. So, it took out a rasp and ran it back and forth across his tongue three times until it was smooth as silk. He waited for his chance to fool the boys.

The next day, everything seemed to be great, so Mama fixed her lunch, kissed the boys, and rushed out the door, leaving her lunch on the table. Around noon, they heard a knock at the door. One of the boys asked, "Mama, what are you doing back now?" In a silky smooth voice came, "It is Mama. I left my lunch." And sure enough, her lunch was on the table. (The alligator saw her leave without it.) "Well Mama, just to be safe, you still need to sing your song, all three shouted".

From outside they heard a beautiful silky smooth voice singing her song…. As they opened the door, the alligator sprang into the house, grabbed the boys, and put them into a croaker sack. As he was about to leave, Mama dashed into the house, picked up a broom, and BAM BAM BAM! She beat the alligator up. He ran away screaming and hollering as he dropped the sack on the floor.

Mama began looking for the boys. They were nowhere to be found. After a moment, she saw the croaker sack on the floor. She opened it, and there were her boys lying at the bottom, not breathing. She began to cry big tears of sadness and love. As her tears fell into the sack, there came a wiggle, and suddenly the oldest boy jumped up, hugged his mom and said, "Oh Mama, your tears of sadness and love brought me back." After a minute, she looked in the bag and the two of them began crying big tears of sadness and love. As their tears fell into the sack, they felt a wiggle and a waggle, and the middle boy jumped up, grabbed his mom and brother and shouted, "Your tears of love and sadness brought me back!!" The three of them checked the sack and saw the youngest boy was not moving. All their tears fell into the sack. After what seemed like forever, the youngest boy began to move. He jumped up, hugged his mom and brothers, and told them their tears of sadness and love had brought him back. Mama whispered a little prayer, "Merci, beaucoup, mon Dieu!!!"

That night the boys did not eat a lot, and could not sleep. Mama knew just the thing to make them feel good. She put them in bed, and sang their favorite lullaby.

"All aboard for blanket bay,

They won't come back til the break of day,

All they need is their little white sheet,

Then you can see their little bare feet.

Their mommy tucks them away in bed, the little boys with the sleepy heads.

Bless mama, bless papa, then they sail away,

All aboard for Blanket Bay."

And just like magic the boys closed their eyes and fell fast asleep.

That old alligator was never heard from again.

The power of love; the magic of three...


The End

# Appendix

Glossary of words

Beignet - a deep-fried pastry usually served with a dusting of powdered sugar.

Croaker sack- a sack made of coarse material such as burlap, used to keep fish alive in water.

Rasp - a coarse file used to shape or sharpen wood or other materials.

Translations of Creole sentences

"Comment sa va?" "How are you?"

"Tres bien, eh vous?" "Very well, and you?"

"Je vais tres bien, merci." "Iam very well, thanks."

"Merci beaucoup, mon Dieu". "Thanks a lot, my God."

QR code. This code will lead readers to a site so that they can actually hear the song that Mama sings each time she leaves, the lullaby she sings at the end of the story and pronunciation of the Creole sentences.

Printed in the United States
by Baker & Taylor Publisher Services